D1383834

Weird the Beard

A portion of proceeds from the sale of Weird the Beard will be donated to First Book, a nonprofit organization that provides new books for children in need. Learn more about their work at www.firstbook.org

Color, image editing and book design by El Yves Margarita

Weird the Beard

Printed in China by Kings Time Printing Press, Ltd.

ISBN 978-0-9829506-2-3
Library of Congress Catalog Number: 2013906757

The display type is set in Akbar, a typeface created and designed by Jon Bernhardt, and is used with his permission.

Second Printing, May 2017

www.octopusinkpress.com

Weird the Beard

OCTOPUS INK
PRESS

Weird the Beard
came from friendly folk.

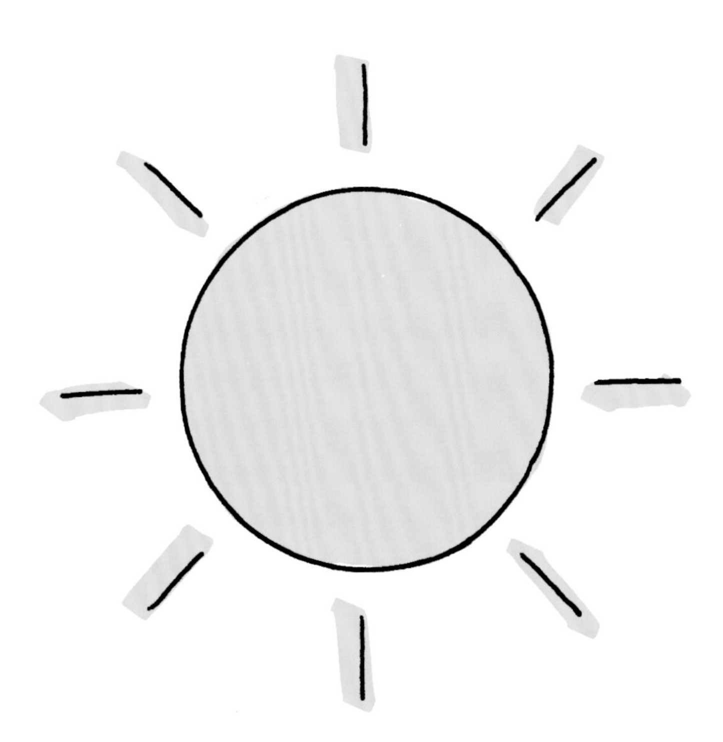

Whenever he met someone
he cracked a joke.

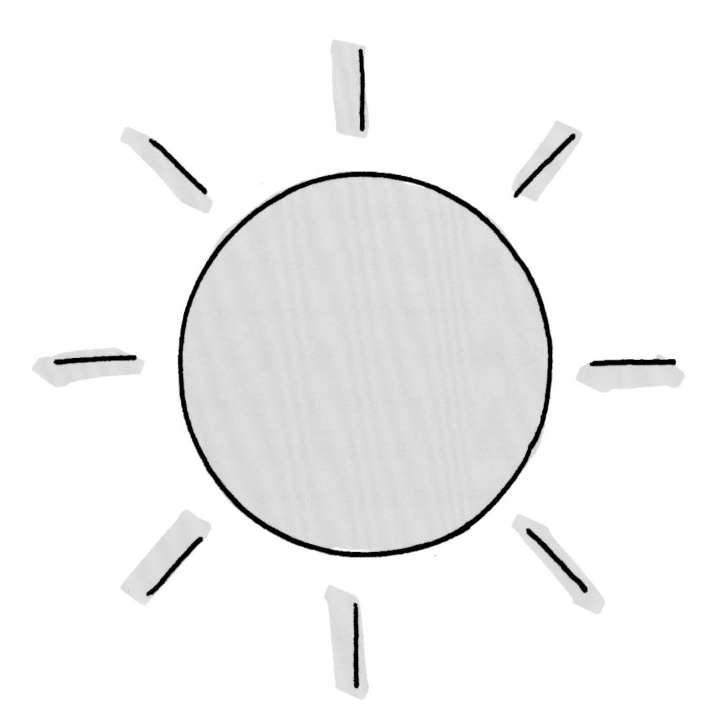

Have you heard the one
about the skunk?

Weird was amusing,
that was true,
Weird is a funny beard
and that's how he grew.

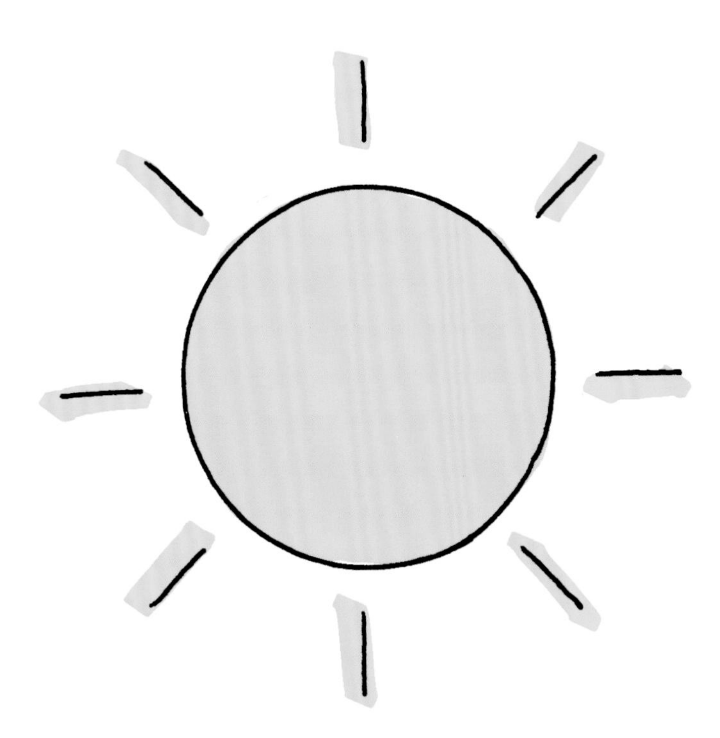

So with a joke to tell
Weird went on his way,
hoping to make
a new friend today.

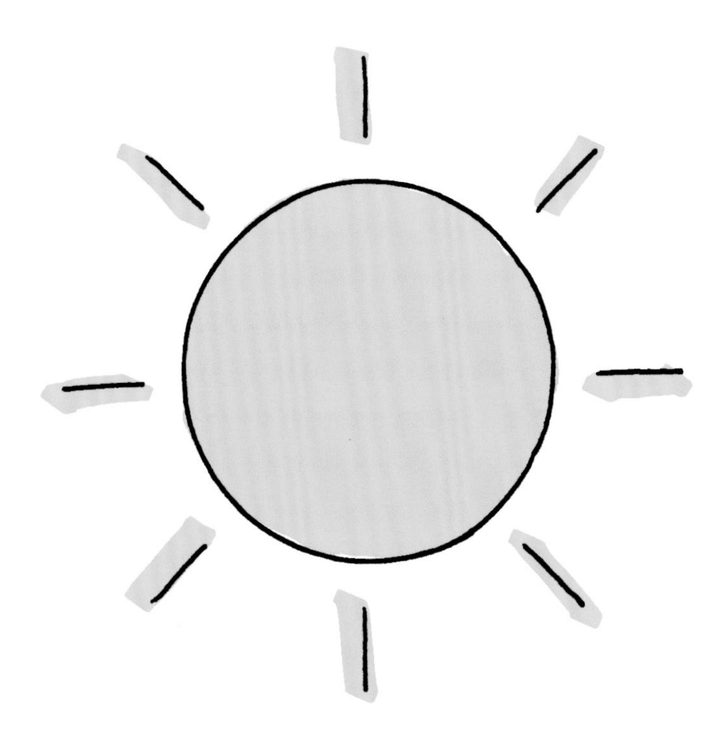

Just then it happened
Weird fell off his face
and dropped on the ground
in a rather strange place.

There he found
in the middle of a ranch
a plastic comb
standing on a branch.

Weird stopped on a whisker
and looked up to say,
"What's happening there?"
in a friendly way.

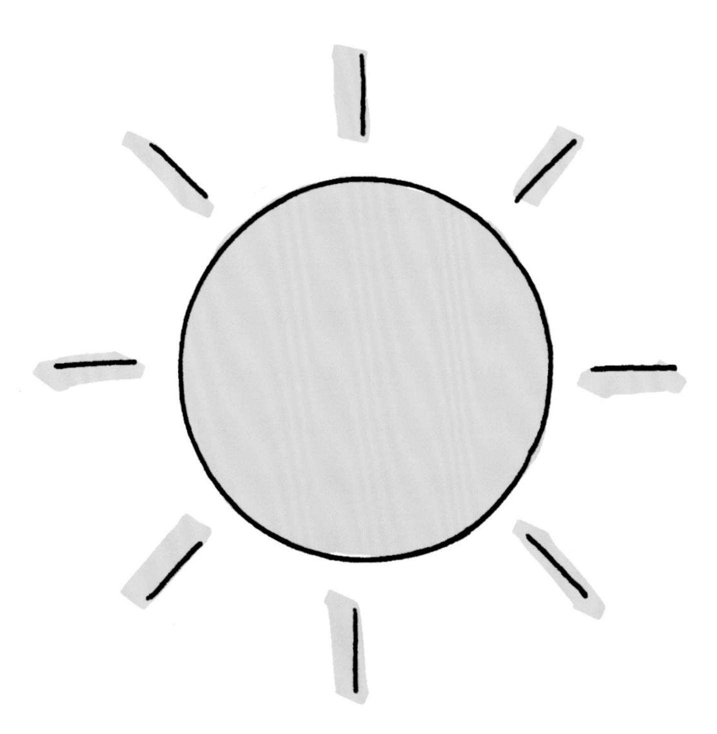

Have you heard the one about the skunk?

The comb looked at Weird
as if to say,
"Yeah, I've heard it."
Then it hurried away.

Yeah, I've heard it.

So with a joke to tell
Weird went on his way,
hoping to make
a new friend today.

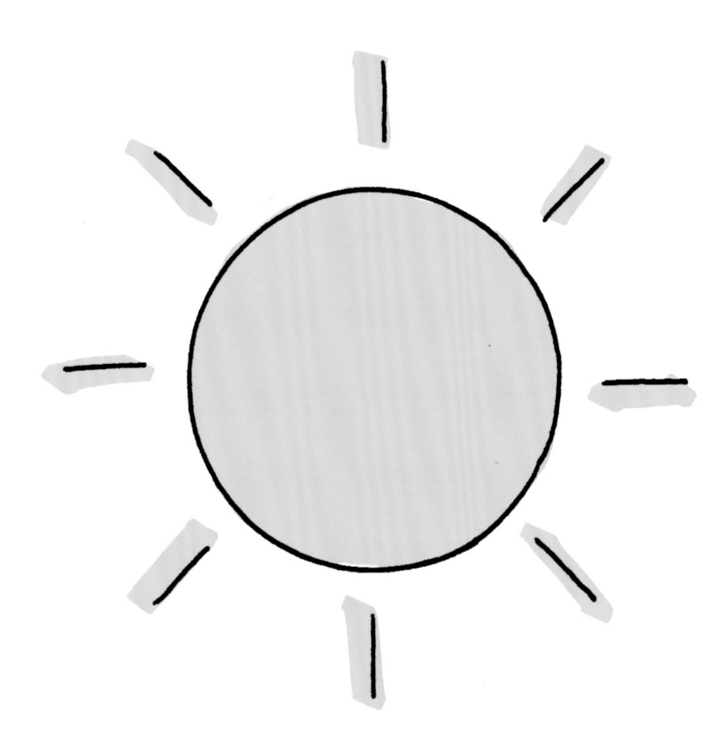

It happened again
Weird fell off his face
and dropped on the ground
in another strange place.

There Weird found,
shiny and brave,
a pair of scissors
in the mouth of a cave.

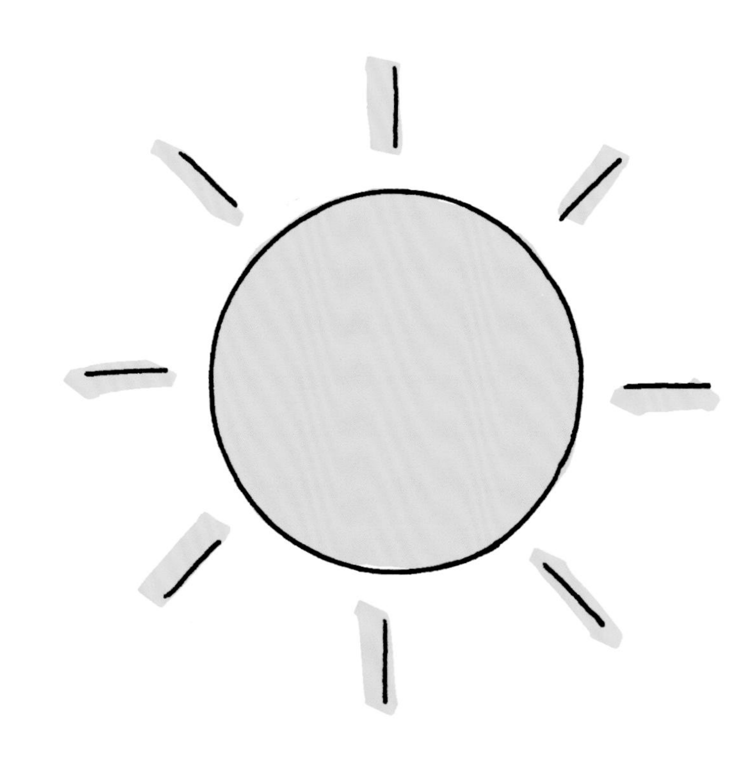

Weird stopped on a whisker
and looked in to say,
"Hello, friend."
Then he joked his weird way.

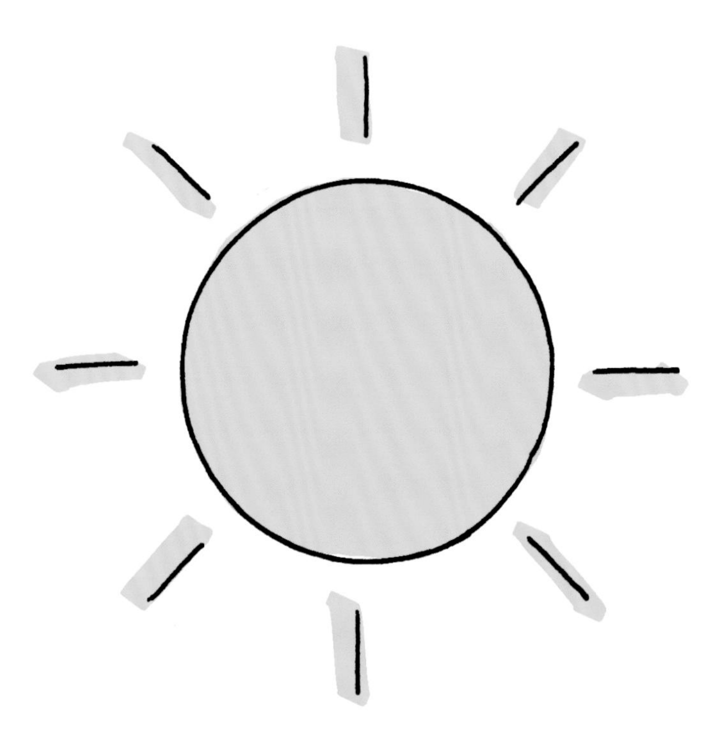

Have you heard the one about the skunk?

The scissors looked at Weird
as if to say,
"About a hundred times."
Then they scurried away.

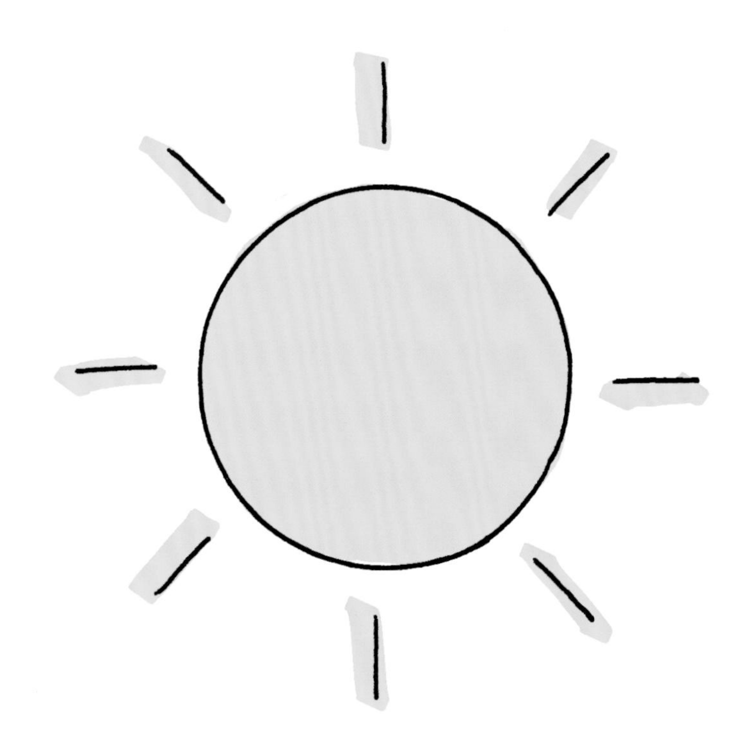

ABOUT A
HUNDRED
TIMES...

So with a joke to tell
Weird went on his way,
hoping to make
a new friend today.

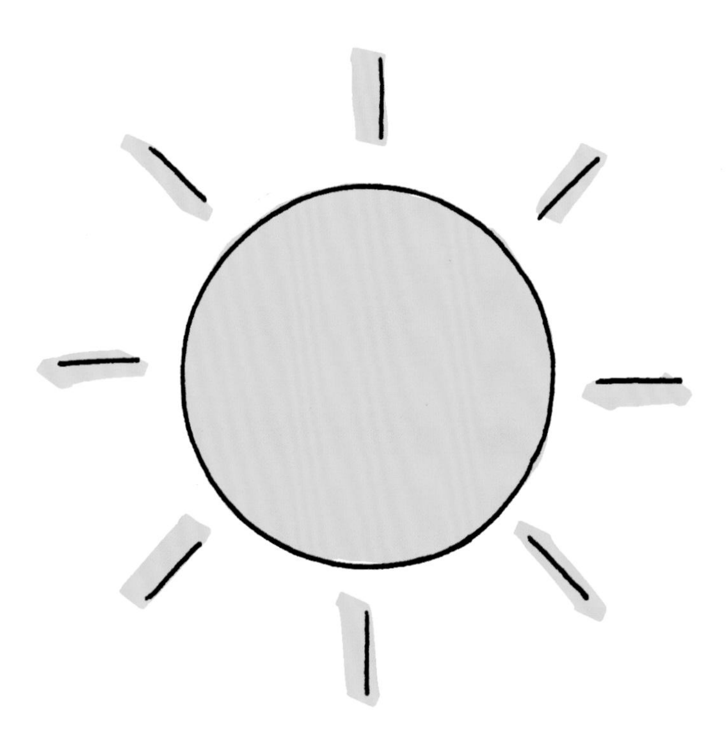

It happened once more
Weird fell off his face
and dropped on the ground
in a final strange place.

There Weird found
someone else to meet,
an electric razor
standing on A Street.

A Street

Weird stopped on a whisker
and looked down to say,
"How do you do?"
Then he joked in his way.

Have you heard the one
about the skunk?

In a quick shave,
below the lash,
Weird the Beard became
Murry the Moustache.

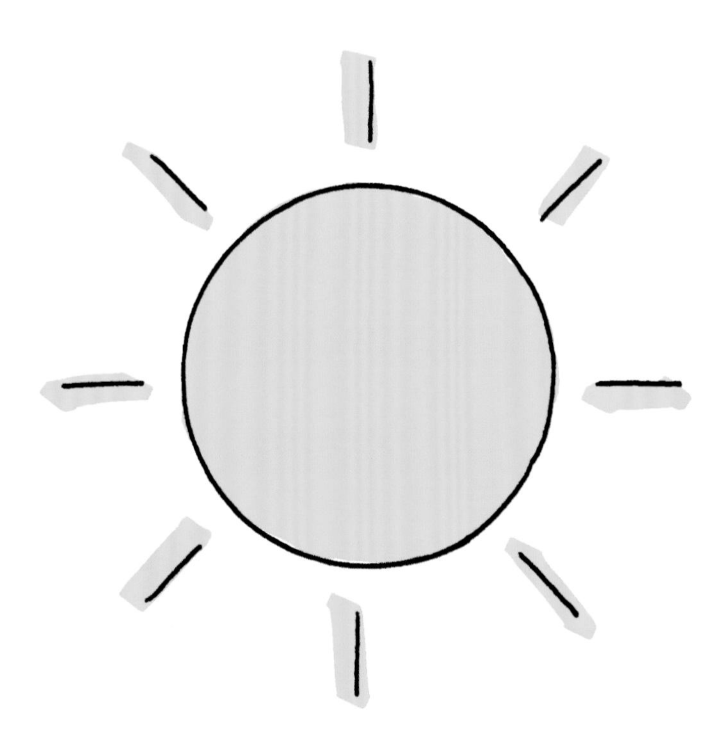

With a grin on his face
as Murry now knew
choose your friends wisely
because they rub off on you.

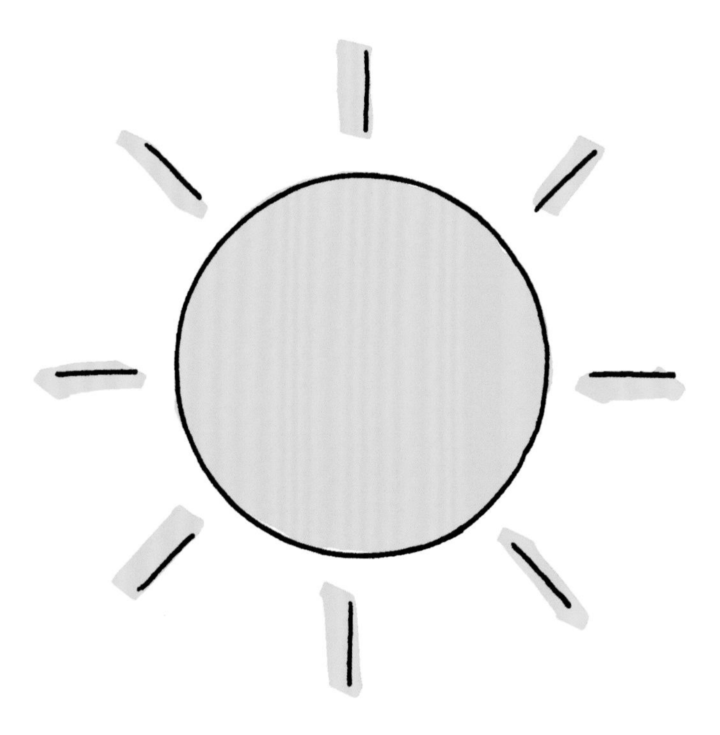

Never mind the skunk joke.

It stinks!

Also from
OCTOPUS INK PRESS

Silly the Seed

Silly the Seed is the heroic adventure of a small seed that grows up to be a beautiful flower. Along the way his acts of friendship and kindness teach and entertain readers of all ages. But when Silly needs help, who will help him?

Lerky the Handturkey

Lerky the Handturkey is the inspiring story of a handturkey whose wise words encourage others to see the bright side. It's the companion to Silly the Seed and Weird the Beard, a wacky tale of friendship and optimism.

Fred and the Monster
Independent Publisher Award Winner, 2015

Fred is afraid of the dark. So is the monster under his bed. One night, Fred's mom does the unthinkable... she turns off the light! Stricken with terror, Fred and the monster must rely on each other for the courage to face their worst fear.

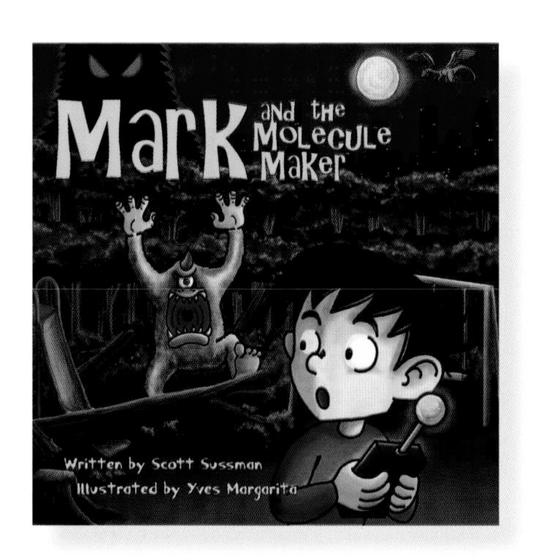

Mark and the Molecule Maker

When Mark enters his father's laboratory and finds the Molecule Maker, he flips the switch and makes a monster. Things go from bad to worse when the creature escapes and Mark races against the sunrise to right the wrong.

Mark and the Molecule Maker 2: The Lightning Jungle

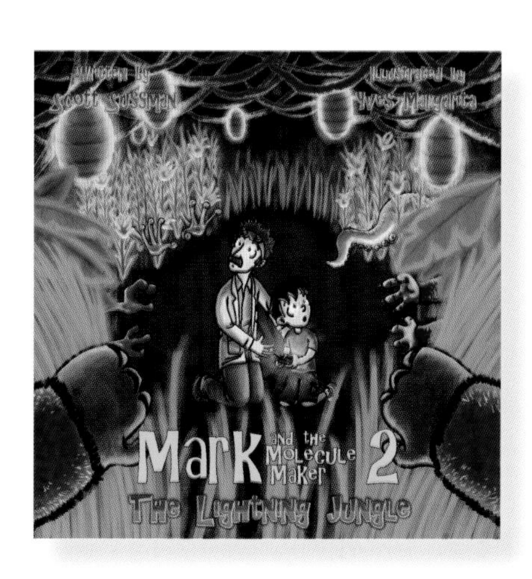

The adventure continues with book two of the Mark and the Molecule Maker trilogy. When the Molecule Maker malfunctions, creating a bunch of mischievous creatures that kidnap Mark's father, Mark races into the lightning jungle on an amazing rescue mission. But will he arrive before it's too late?

Mark and the Molecule Maker 3: The Underground Mountain

In the thrilling conclusion to the Mark and the Molecule Maker trilogy, the chase is on when a cunning monster steals the Molecule Maker. In a desperate attempt to retrieve the extraordinary invention, Mark and his father must risk their lives on the treacherous underground mountain, where danger lurks behind every boulder and hides inside every hole.

THE SHINING ADVENTURES OF
SHELPA MCSTORM
SCOTT SUSSMAN
ILLUSTRATIONS BY NOEL TUAZON